EX LIBRIS

THIS BOOK BELONGS TO

FOR MY MOTHER

Lani Yamamoto

STÍNA

V&A Publishing

tína didn't like the cold. She couldn't
eat ice cream, she wouldn't touch metal,
and she never wore skirts without tights
AND socks that covered her knees.

In summer, Stína easily avoided swimming pools and cool evening breezes, but the only place she truly felt safe from a possible chill was at home, in bed, under her big, white, goose-down duvet.

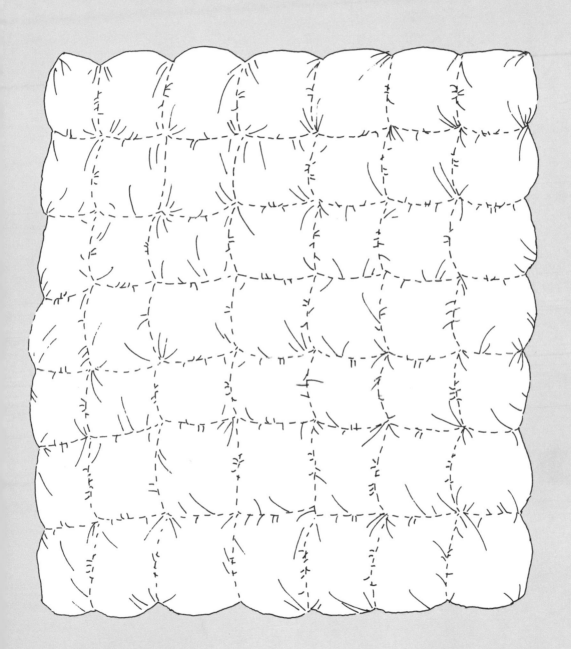

In winter, Stína simply stayed at home. With a bit of early planning, she was ready for every situation imaginable.

So one morning, late last autumn, when Stína first saw her breath, she calmly took a step back inside and shut the door.

Days began with hot oatmeal and books by the fire.
Days ended snug in bed playing hide-and-seek with the moon.

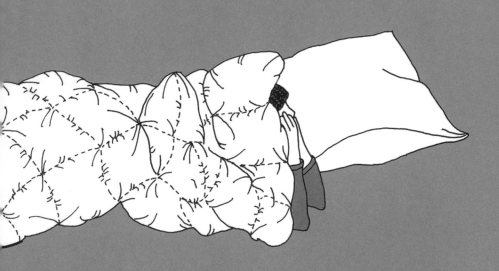

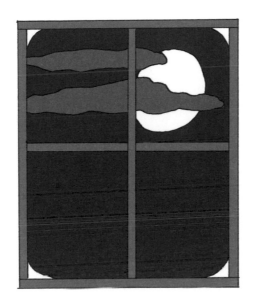

In between, Stína came up with new and improved ways
to protect herself from the cold.

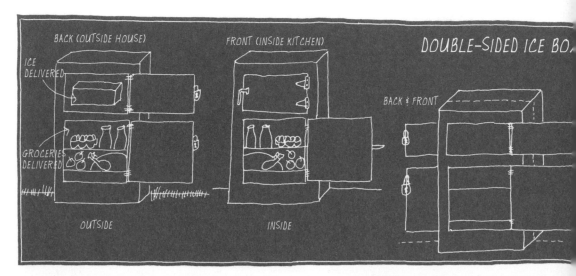

BACK (OUTSIDE HOUSE)

FRONT (INSIDE KITCHEN)

DOUBLE-SIDED ICE BO...

ICE DELIVERED

GROCERIES DELIVERED

OUTSIDE

INSIDE

BACK & FRONT

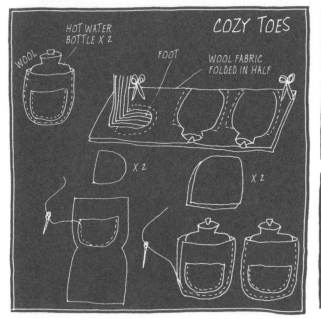

COZY TOES

HOT WATER BOTTLE X 2

WOOL

FOOT

WOOL FABRIC FOLDED IN HALF

X 2

X 2

MITTEN CUP WARMER

SINGLE MITTEN

UNRAVEL PAST THUMB

RE-KNIT EDGE

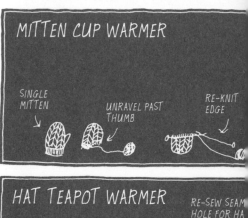

HAT TEAPOT WARMER

RE-SEW SEAM
HOLE FOR HA...

OLD HAT

UNRAVEL SEAM

TI...
KN...

SEAM

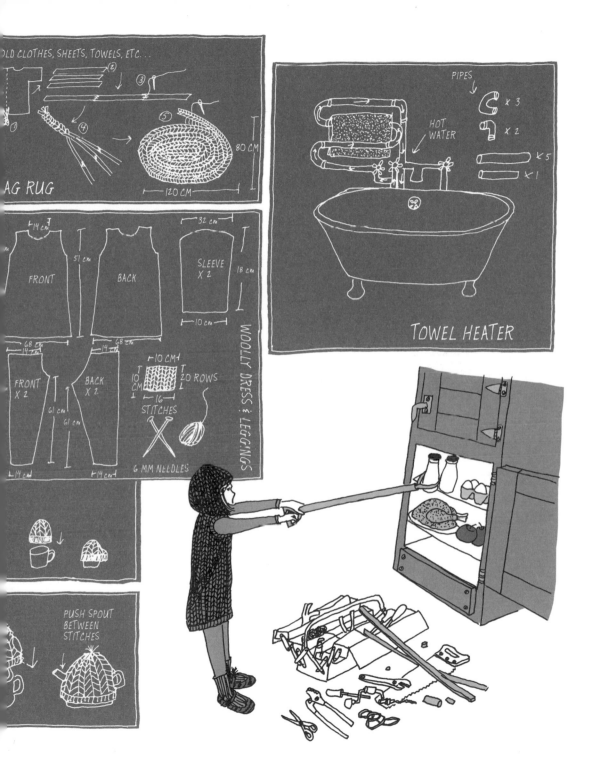

She was so busy at first that she hardly noticed the kids playing outside, but as the days came and went, Stína became more curious about them.

Wasn't the wind blowing right through their sweaters?

How did they keep snow out of their mittens and boots?

What did snowflakes taste like?

It got colder and darker and Stína had to do more
and more to keep warm.

It became harder to get out of bed.

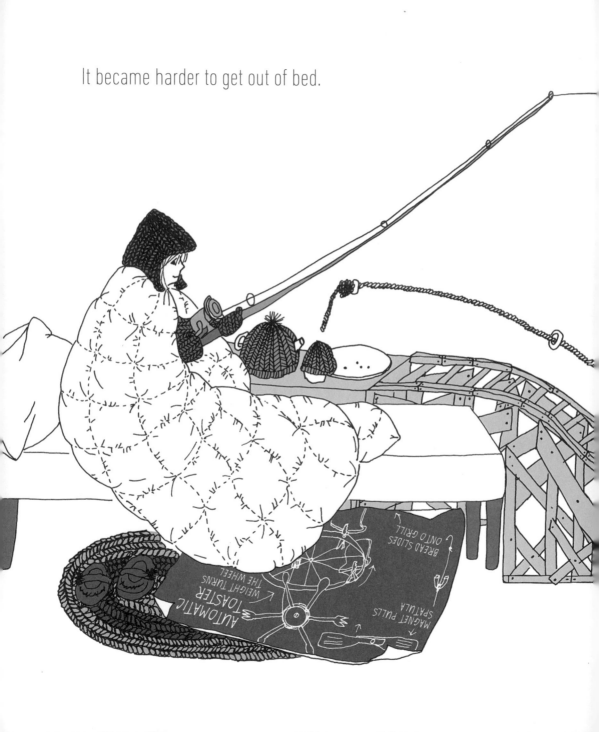

Every morning the duvet felt bigger and heavier, until one day
she couldn't lift it at all. Exhausted from the effort,
she fell into a deep, dreamless sleep.

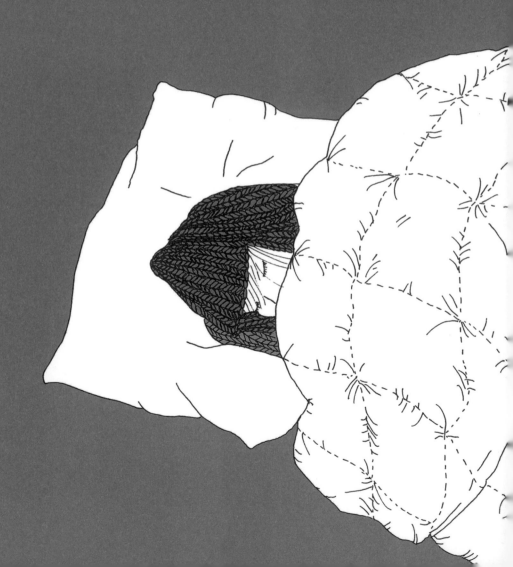

When Stína finally opened her eyes, she had no idea
how much time had passed. The room was dark and still,
but outside the wind howled and the snow whirled.

Stína shivered under the duvet. She heard voices blow
by the window and then a loud pounding on the door.

With all her might, she pulled the duvet around her and hurried
toward the door. She braced herself and turned the knob.

A gust of wind blew the kids inside.

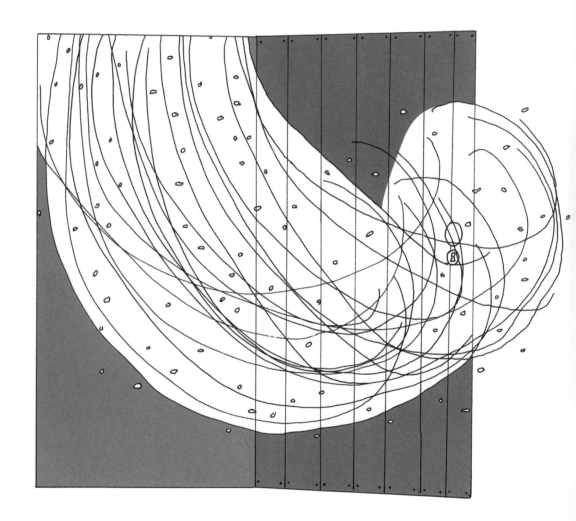

Another slammed the door behind them.

Stína rushed to get a fire going, but to her great surprise,
the kids were rushing out of their things to cool off.

It was very quiet.

"Waffles?" asked Stína.

The kids told Stína their plan to make a snowball so big it would last all summer and taught her how to whistle with her fingers.

Stína showed the kids how to knit without needles and gave them her recipe for the best hot cocoa they'd ever tasted.

EVERLASTINC

17 M

FINGER WHISTLING

① MAKE A TRIANGLE WITH YOUR FINGERS LIKE THIS:

② OPEN YOUR MOUTH. CURL YOUR LIPS IN AND ROLL YOUR TONGUE BACK AND UP, PRESSING THE TIP AGAINST THE ROOF OF YOUR MOUTH.

③ PUSH YOUR FINGERTIPS AGAINST YOUR TONGUE, RESTING YOUR FINGERS ON YOUR BOTTOM LIP. WITH YOUR LIPS STILL CURLED IN, CLOSE YOUR MOUTH AROUND YOUR FINGERS SO THERE IS ONLY A SMALL TRIANGLE-SHAPED HOLE IN FRONT THAT THE AIR CAN COME THROUGH. BLOW HARD. KEEP MOVING YOUR LIPS AND FINGERS AROUND UNTIL YOU GET A CLEAR SOUND.

KNITTING WITHOUT NEEDLES

1. WRAP THE YARN TWICE AROUND YOUR THUMB. TUCK THE END UNDER SO IT STAYS IN PLACE.

2. WEAVE THE YARN BETWEEN YOUR FINGERS, STARTING BEHIND YOUR POINTER FINGER AND BACK AGAIN, ENDING IN FRONT OF YOUR POINTER FINGER.

4. PULL THE BOTTOM LOOP OVER THE TOP LOOP AND OVER THE TOP OF YOUR POINTER FINGER.

5. HOLDING THE YARN ACROSS YOUR FINGERS, PULL THE BOTTOM LOOP OVER THE YARN AND OVER THE TOP OF YOUR MIDDLE FINGER. DO THE SAME FOR THE REST OF THE FINGERS.

...TING WILL BUILD UP ON THE BACK ...D.

8. WHEN YOU WANT TO STOP UNDO THE THUMB LOOPS AND TAKE THE REST OF THE LOOPS OFF EACH FINGER ONTO A PENCIL.

...JA'S HOT COCOA*

...TABLESPOON UNSWEETENED COCOA POWDER, 1 TABLESPOON SUGAR, 1 CUP OF MILK, AND 2 SQUARES OF YOUR FAVORITE CHOCOLATE IN A POT. COOK OVER A MEDIUM HEAT, STIRRING UNTIL EVERYTHING IS MIXED TOGETHER AND IT IS JUST ABOUT TO BOIL. TAKE THE POT OFF THE HEAT AND STIR IN THE TINIEST PINCH OF SALT. POUR INTO A CUP AND SPOON SOME WHIPPED CREAM ON TOP.

THIS MAKES 1 CUP OF HOT COCOA.

*PLEASE CHECK WITH AN ADULT BEFORE YOU BEGIN.

They made up songs until the storm blew over, then said their reluctant goodbyes.

That night, Stína couldn't sleep.

Nothing made sense. She was cold inside where it was warm,
but the kids had been warm outside where it was cold.
She had tried everything she could imagine to stay warm
but still she felt colder every day.

So Stína imagined something she'd never imagined
she'd imagine, and got to work.

The sun had not come up yet when Stína finished,
but she couldn't wait. She opened the door and
stepped out into the dim early morning.

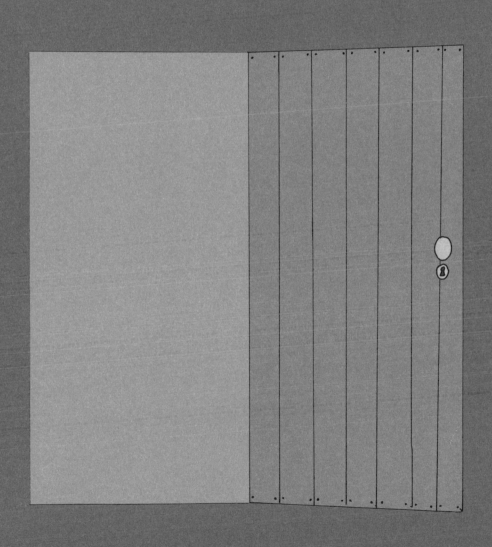

It was still and cold. The air was icy, but she hardly noticed.
A gentle snow was falling and Stína was trying
to catch the flakes on her tongue.

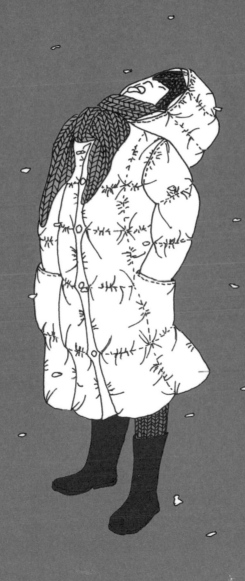

Breathless from running and laughing, Stína was warming up,
and as the sun rose, she thought of her new friends
and felt even warmer still.

KNITTING WITHOUT NEEDLES

1. WRAP THE YARN TWICE AROUND YOUR THUMB. TUCK THE END UNDER SO IT STAYS IN PLACE.

2. WEAVE THE YARN BETWEEN YOUR FINGERS. STARTING BEHIND YOUR POINTER FINGER AND BACK AGAIN, EN IN FRONT OF YOUR POINTER FINGER.

3. WRAP THE YARN ONCE AGAIN AROUND YOUR POINTER FINGER SO YOU HAVE TWO LOOPS AND THE YARN LIES ACROSS THE FRONT OF YOUR FINGERS.

4. PULL THE BOTTOM LOOP OVER THE TOP LOOP AN D OVER THE TOP OF YOUR POINTER FINGER.

5. HOLDING THE YARN ACROSS YOUR FINGERS, PULL THE BOTTOM LOOP OVER THE YARN AND OVER THE TOP OF YOUR MIDDLE FINGER. DO THE SAME FOR THE REST OF THE FINGERS.

6. WHEN YOU ARE DONE WITH YOUR PINKY, BRING THE YARN BACK ACROSS YOUR FINGERS TOWARD YOUR THUMB. REPEAT STEPS 5 AND 6 FOR ALL YOUR FINGERS (EXCEPT YOUR THUMB).

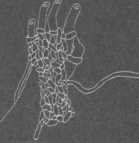

7. THE KNITTING WILL BUILD UP ON THE BACK OF YOUR HAND.

8. WHEN YOU WANT TO STOP, UND THE THUMB LOOPS AND TAKE THE REST OF THE LOOPS OFF EAC FINGER ONTO A PENCIL.

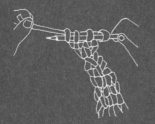

9–10. YOU CAN KEEP THE KNITTING LIKE THIS UNTIL YOU WANT TO KNIT SOME MORE. OR, IF YOU ARE FINISHED, CUT THE YARN (LEAVING ABOUT 30 CM ON THE END), PUT THE END THROUGH THE LOOPS, TAKE THE PENCIL AWAY, AND PULL GENTLY. TIE A KNOT.

STINA'S HOT COCOA*

PUT 1 TABLESPOON UNSWEETENED COCOA POWDER,
1 TABLESPOON SUGAR, 1 CUP OF MILK,
AND 2 SQUARES OF YOUR FAVORITE CHOCOLATE
IN A POT. COOK OVER A MEDIUM HEAT, STIRRING
UNTIL EVERYTHING IS MIXED TOGETHER AND IT IS JUST
ABOUT TO BOIL. TAKE THE POT OFF THE HEAT AND STIR
IN THE TINIEST PINCH OF SALT. POUR INTO
A CUP AND SPOON SOME WHIPPED CREAM ON TOP.

THIS MAKES 1 CUP OF HOT COCOA.

Lani Yamamoto
STÍNA

First published by V&A Publishing, 2015
Victoria and Albert Museum
South Kensington
London SW7 2RL
www.vandapublishing.com

Distributed in North America by Abrams,
ən imprint of ABRAMS

ı. ınal title: **STÍNA STÓRASÆNG**
By Lana Yamamoto

First edition published in Icelandic 2013
by Crymogea ehf., Reykjavík.
© 2013 Lani Yamamoto

This edition is published by V&A Publishing under
license from Crymogea. www.crymogea.is

The moral right of the author(s) has been asserted.

Hardback edition
ISBN 978 1 85177 858 4

Library of Congress Control Number 2015947206

10 9 8 7 6 5 4 3 2 1
2019 2018 2017 2016 2015

A catalogue record for this book is available
from the British Library.

Every effort has been made to seek permission
to reproduce those images whose copyright does
not reside with the V&A, and we are grateful to the
individuals and institutions who have assisted in this
task. Any omissions are entirely unintentional, and the
details should be addressed to V&A Publishing.

Designer: Ármann Agnarsson

Printed in Slovenia

V&A Publishing
Supporting the world's leading
museum of art and design,
the Victoria and Albert
Museum, London